D

i

D1415055

Hidden Hunters!

Adapted by Steve Behling
Illustrated by MJ Illustrations

A Random House PICTUREBACK® Book

Random House 🏠 New York

Jurassic World Franchise © 2021 Universal City Studios LLC and Amblin Entertainment, Inc. Series © 2021 DreamWorks Animation LLC. All Rights Reserved. Published in the United States by Random House Children's Books, a division of Penguin Random House LLC, 1745 Broadway, New York, NY 10019, and in Canada by Penguin Random House Canada Limited, Toronto. Pictureback, Random House, and the Random House colophon are registered trademarks of Penguin Random House LLC.

rhcbooks.com

Educators and librarians, for a variety of teaching tools, visit us at RHTeachersLibrarians.com

ISBN 978-0-593-30429-7 (trade) — ISBN 978-0-593-30430-3 (ebook)
Printed in the United States of America

10 9 8 7 6 5 4 3 2 1

Random House Children's Books supports the First Amendment and celebrates the right to read.

Camp Cretaceous was a brand-new camp where kids could spend the summer with dinosaurs. But one day, when the dinosaurs went on a rampage, the island was evacuated—and the kids got left behind! Since then, one camper, Yasmina, hurt her ankle; another—Ben—didn't make it. Now Darius, Brooklynn, Kenji, Yasmina, and Sammy were trying to survive.

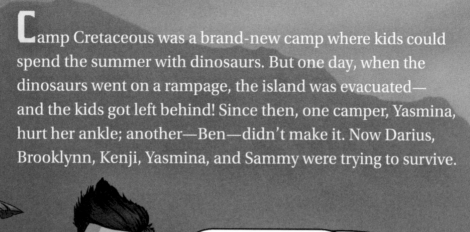

A campfire! Maybe someone had come to rescue them! Excited, the kids raced through the jungle.

But suddenly—*ROAR!* A Ceratosaurus came crashing toward them—and it looked hungry!

The Ceratosaurus nearly reached them
before they were pushed out of harm's way.
A flare went off, its bright light scaring the
dinosaur away.

"I'm Mitch," a man said as the kids
looked up to see who had saved them.

"My better half here is Tiff. We're ecotourists!"
Mitch said.

"That's a fancy way of saying we travel to exotic
places to photograph rare animals," Tiff said. She
and Mitch were exploring Jurassic World with the
help of their guide, Hap.

The campers were thrilled to have been found.

Mitch and Tiff brought the kids to their luxury campsite, where they had actual food! As the kids told them all about the dinosaurs, the ecotourists explained that their rescue ship would soon pick the kids up.

Darius was excited to talk dinosaurs with Mitch. In fact, everyone seemed relaxed except Brooklynn.

Mitch and Tiff wanted to see dinosaurs right away.
The new group didn't get very far before they ran into
some hungry Compsognathuses!

Thinking fast, Darius waved a granola bar at the
Compys. When he threw it into a bush, the dinosaurs
took the bait and dove after it!

Meanwhile, Brooklynn and Kenji stayed behind at the camp. Brooklynn wanted to find out more about Mitch and Tiff—and especially Hap.

When Brooklynn tried to enter Hap's yurt, an alarm blared.

"You! Stay away from the yurt!" Hap hollered.
The kids backed off. Now they were sure this guy was up to something.

Darius took Mitch and Tiff to a grassy valley where the Brachiosauruses grazed. He called out to the dinosaurs with a loud Brachiosaurus call—and the giant creatures answered! The ecotourists were impressed.

"If you think *this* is cool, there's one more place we could go," Darius said.

The watering hole!

Back at camp, Brooklynn and Kenji tried to escape Hap. They thought he was trying to hurt them! The kids moved fast through the jungle, but Hap was faster. He managed to get ahead of the campers and block their path.

"You have no idea who you're dealing with . . . ," Hap began.

But before he could finish, something whacked him with
a tree branch. Brooklynn and Kenji looked up in surprise.
Standing there before them was Ben!

Ben was alive! And his dinosaur pal, Bumpy, was by his side.
"What? You've never seen a ghost before?" Ben said, smiling.

Hap rubbed his head. "You kids have to trust me," he said. "I'm trying to save your lives!"

Hap revealed what Darius soon saw for himself—that Mitch and Tiff weren't really ecotourists. They were hunters! They were paying Hap to catch dinosaurs, not take photos. But Hap refused to endanger the kids.

If the kids wanted to rescue their friends from Mitch and Tiff, they had to trust Hap. Together, they found an abandoned garage. But a trio of angry Baryonyxes attacked! Before the dinosaurs could do any damage, Brooklynn and Kenji escaped on a motorcycle with Hap, while Ben rode Bumpy.

The Baryonyxes ran fast, coming closer and closer to the kids. Hap stared at them and realized what he had to do.

"We all make mistakes," Hap said. "I'm making up for mine now." Then he leaped from the sidecar, holding a stun spear in his hands.

Meanwhile, Kenji and Brooklynn were surprised to see Yasmina run from the jungle. She told them that Mitch and Tiff had taken Sammy and Darius prisoner! The hunters thought they were forcing Darius to lead them to the watering hole. But really, he was taking them to Jurassic World's Main Street . . . where the fearsome T. rex now lived!

Darius and Sammy arrived on Main Street with Mitch and Tiff. Kenji, Brooklynn, Yasmina, and Ben followed, racing to turn the power to Jurassic World back on.

But as the Park came to life, the sounds and lights attracted the attention of the ravenous T. rex, who went after Darius and Sammy!

The campers had an idea. Brooklynn, Kenji, Yasmina, and Ben activated a hologram of a T. rex, which confused the real dinosaur. Darius and Sammy were safe! But Mitch and Tiff got away and were heading straight for the watering hole. The kids would have to act fast to save the dinosaurs.

The campers came up with a clever plan. They looked around for vehicles and found a 6x4.

With Bumpy's help, they led the dinosaurs away from the watering hole. Now there wouldn't be any creatures for Mitch and Tiff to hunt!

The thundering herd headed straight for Mitch and Tiff. The couple just managed to leap into the safety of a tree before being trampled.

The dinosaurs passed, and Mitch jumped down. But he accidentally stepped on a dinosaur trap that Hap had set earlier.

WHOOSH! Mitch was whisked into the air, captured.

Leaving Mitch behind, Tiff raced ahead to the boat. She jumped aboard and took off before Darius could stop her. "I win!" she said, taunting him. "I'm out of here!"

But Tiff's plans were ruined because there were dinosaurs aboard the boat! The dinosaurs attacked, and the boat ran aground.

"So . . . what now?" Kenji asked. "Try to find another distress beacon?"

"No," Darius said. "We're done waiting for someone to rescue us. It's time we found our *own* way off the island!"